The Name of this Book is Named

SMARTYPANTS

(Pete in School)

by

Maira Kalman

G.P. PUTNAM'S SONS . NEW YORK

THNAKS
BIG to NANCY PAULSEN
and
The STUPENDOUS KIDS OF
P.S. 234, P.S. 198, CITY + COUNTRY
ALL IN NEW YORK CITY, NY
AND MUCHLY TO
EVA ANDERSON, and
ALFRED MENDOZA and
ELIZABETH JOHNSON.

PRESIDENT

VICE PRESIDENT

SECRETARY OF THE HAIR PULLING CLUB.

My Name is Poppy Wise.
BEARD
WAS SO LONG

This is
my BROTHER
Mookie,
who I sometimes call
ShMookie ScAlandRoopy.

AND this IS OUR DOG,
PETE.
A WONDERFUL DOG.
WHO WONDERS ABOUT
ONLY ONE Thing.
EaTINg WhaT
HE
SHOULD
NOT.
He aLReady ATe

an ACCORDION

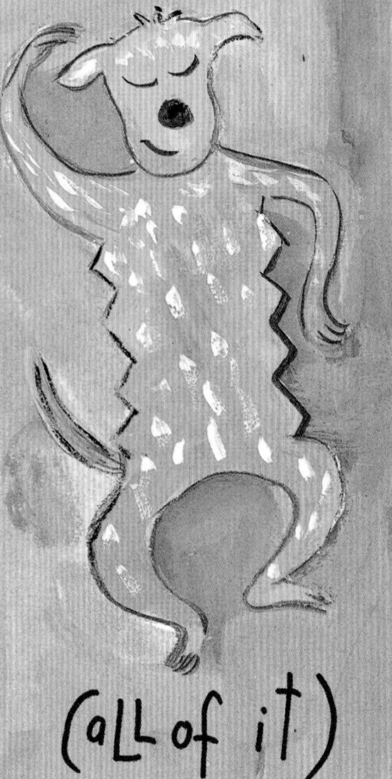

(aLL of it)

MooKIE'S STINKY SNeaKeR

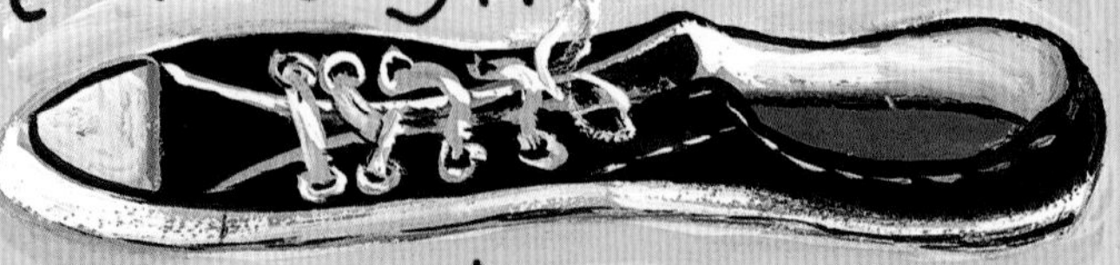

AND
The UNDERPANTS OF
My UNCLe ROCKY.

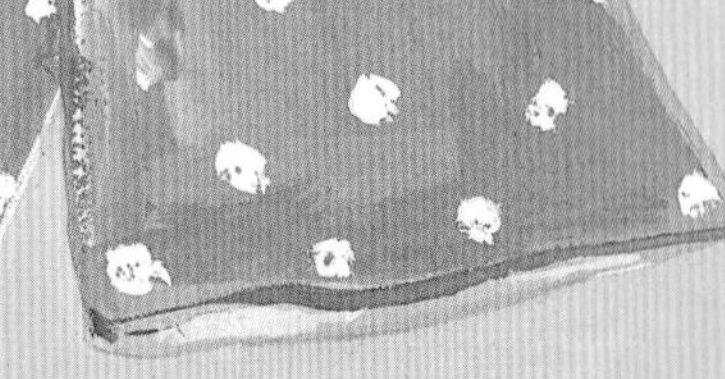

UGGH!

BUT IT DID NOT STOP There.

HE ATE THE REMOTE CONTROL
AND WE HAD TO PRESS HIS
STOMACH TO TURN THE CHANNELS.

WORLD'S LARGEST CHEESE
"BIG DEAL. I'VE SEEN BIGGER."

AND ON SUMMER VACATION
when we WENT TO VISIT
The WORLD'S LARGEST CHEESE, he ATE IT!
He is INCORRIGIBLE. He IS PETE.

Now the SWEET SUMMER is over.
I MUST CLIMB DOWN FROM my Leafy Tree
and Go To SCHOOL.
SCHOOL.
YOU NEVER KNOW
when YOU WILL Be STUPID
IN FRONT OF The WHOLE CLASS
(and SOMEONE WILL whisper, "WHAT an IDIOT").
YOU NEVER KNOW when Someone
WILL LAUGH at The UGLY SWEATER
YOUR AUNT SENT YOU.
AND YOU NEVER KNOW when there WILL
Be a POP QUIZ
BUT YOU KNOW There
WILL Be ONE and you think,
I HATE
SCHOOL!

But then something
wonderful happens,
like you win the
Punchball game or
you understand long division
or you write a story with
absolutely no spelling
mistakes and the teacher
writes BRAVO or
it's Friday and you get
ice cream for lunch
and you get that
tingly melty
feeling and
then you think,
I LOVE
SCHOOL!
NUTHATCH

Mookie and I walk to school with Doreen Parsley and Butch Barker, who kicks his lucky pebble all the way to school.

The pebble waits patiently in Butch's pocket until school is out.

the pebble enlarged 10x

Pete stays home alone.

WHY?

ONCE, DURING SHOW-and-TELL, BUTCH BROUGHT HIS SNAKE, JUDY. JUDY SLITHERED AWAY AND COULDN'T BE FOUND.

EVERYONE WENT NUTS.

(THEY FOUND JUDY CURLED UP IN DOREEN'S BOOT. UGGH.) SINCE THEN THE RULE IS NO PETS IN SCHOOL. THERE ARE RULES FOR EVERYTHING IN SCHOOL. SOMETIMES THEY MAKE YOU WANT TO YELL at SOMEBODY.

BUT NEVER AT MISS HONEYBEE.
MISS EDWINA HONEYBEE IS OUR PRINCIPAL.
SHE HAS BOUNCY HAIR AND A
LITTLE SONGBIRD
NAMED
MILTON.
(MILTON IS NOT
A PET. HE IS A
MILTON.)
MISS HONEY BEE
IS A HONEY.
SHE SAYS THINGS
LIKE
"MISTAKES
BRING GOOD"
AND
"CHIN
UP"
THE DOOR OF
MISS
HONEYBEE

Speaking of Math (NOT), our Teacher is
Mr. Grompi Spitzer,
the GRIBBLIEST
Teacher on
EARTH.
He Lost His
PATIENCE in a
SUITCASE
in Topeka,
and now
when He is
NERVOUS,
His Hair
Twitches
and his
Nostrils
Get
HUGE.

We are STUDYING I N F I N I T Y, WHICH is the Longest thing You can Never See the END OF Because it has NO END (like this math class).
MR. SPITZER asks an IMPOSSIBLE QUESTION.
If you know the ANSWER (Like Mookie the Math WHIZ), You wave your hand FRANTICALLY and say, "OOH. OOH OOH pick ME."
"THIS IS SOPORIFIC."
"THIS STUFF MAKES MY EYES CROSS."

BUT, IF YOU HAVE NOT DONE A STITCH OF WORK (like POPPY NOT SO WISE) AND DON'T WANT TO BE CALLED ON, YOU MUST

AVOID EYE CONTACT

at all COSTS AND START SHARPENING YOUR PENCILS WITH FRANTIC FERVOR,

which is WHAT I WAS DOING when There was a MEDIUM-SIZED RUMPUS, AND

in Ran
PETE
(who was
Lonely at Home)
and Before
you could say
QUADRATIC
EQUATION,
he ate
the
BLACKBOARD
the
FRACTIONS
IN A BOX MARKED
FRACTIONS
AND
MR. SPITZER'S
PANTS.

RULES
1. DON'T DO IT.
2. I SAID DON'T.
3. I MEAN IT.
4. STOP IT.
5. RIGHT NOW.
MORE RULES
1. QUIET.
2. SILENCE.
3. DON'T TALK.
4. DON'T SCRATCH.
5. DON'T WIGGLE.
6. DON'T MOVE AT ALL.
FRACTIONS
3 × 3 = 8 X
4 × 2 = 5 X
2 × 2 = 9 X
"I have ANTS in MY PANTS."
MR. SPITZER WAS NOT HAPPY
and VERY ANGRY and
10 X 10 FURIOUS
(WHICH IS
100%
FURIOUS).

PETE RAN INTO MISS MAGMA'S SCIENCE CLASS.

MOOD CH AN GES
HAPPY
SAD
MAD
CONFUSED
WE ARE STUDYING CHANGE. YOU CAN CHANGE YOUR MIND. YOU MUST CHANGE YOUR SOCKS EVERY DAY. The Seasons CHANGE. Liquids CHANGE into SOLIDS and
"I AM A CLOUD."
FUNNELS and TEST TUBES and MICROSCOPES can CHANGE FROM VISIBLE to INVISIBLE when PETE EATS THEM.
MISS MAGMA is BOILING MAD, which Means Her TEMPERATURE HAS SHOT UP to 212°F. MISS MAGMA HAS A MELTDOWN!
"I'M SHOCKED"
GO AHEAD. MEASURE SOMETHING. YOUR TONGUE PERHAPS.
1
2
3
4
5
6
7
8
9
10

We change rooms FAST and take PETE to Miss Lulu Crumple's art class. Art is where there are no rules.
"NO ART FOR ME."
Miss Crumple is an ARTIST with an OPEN MIND, so when PETE EATS all the CRAYONS, Miss Crumple is TICKLED PINK and says, "I have never seen such a colorful dog."

We race into Mr. Moosebrugger's orchestra, where Pete eats ALL the instruments, including the tubas. Mookie was singing with joy because he had not practiced his violin all summer.

LUNCHTIME. YAAAY. We SCReaM and YeLL and FOOD FaLLS OUT OF OUR MOUTHS. We have SO MUCH FUN.

The teachers DON'T. They SIT Together and talk aBOUT HEADACHES and WHY They are NOT FAR FAR AWAY cLIMBING MOUNT Everest.

AND whiLe TWITCHY SPITZY was getTing a Cup of tea, Pete gOBBLed up His Liverwurst Sandwich and His PANTS (again).

MR. SPITZER WAS "AGOG AT A DOG RUNNING AMOK AND CAUSING HAVOC. A RULE IS A RULE. NO DOG IN SCHOOL. PETE MUST GO GO GO GO GO GO"

(AND THEN WE HEAR THE DREADED WORDS)

"TO THE PRINCIPAL'S OFFICE."

When PETE got there, Miss Honeybee was called away on an EMERGENCY. (Someone had thrown magnets in the toilet.)

The room was quiet except for the sweet singing of MILTON.

Pete looked around.

He saw many things that looked DELICIOUS. There was an UMBRELLA. There was a TUMBLEWEED That Had TUMBLED FROM SWEETWATER, TEXAS. But PETE was NOT interested in Those Things. PETE GOBBLED UP...

(NO, NOT MILTON! ARE YOU CRAZY?) He ATE the 26-VOLUME ENCYCLOPEDIA ABOUT EVERYTHING THERE IS TO KNOW ABOUT EVERYTHING by PROFESSOR ZELDA PEABODY.

How They Expect you to Learn
EVERYThing is a MYSTERY
To Me.
I Know when I FEEL SICK.
I Know how to spell ONOMATOPOEIA.
I Know how to FLIP a Fried EGG.
I Know how to play the UKeLeLe.
I Know Many Many Things.
BUT, I don't Know
EVERYThiNG.
Is such a thing Possible?
RINGS
and
SLINKYS
TiME
UKELELE
VOLCANO
whistle.
YAWNING

That night Pete was curled up in the corner while we were doing our homework.

Mookie asked, "What galaxy is our solar system in?" I was doing my own work. I was busy and cranky and I didn't want to help Mookie.

"Poppy, what galaxy is our solar system in?"

"Mookie, Leave me ALONE."

From far away, Pete sighed, smacked his lips and said, "The Milky Way."

"Excuse Me?" we said.

Pete Repeated, "The EARTH is the third PLANET FROM the SUN in our NINE-PLANET SOLAR SYSTEM, which is PART OF The MILKY WAY galaxy."

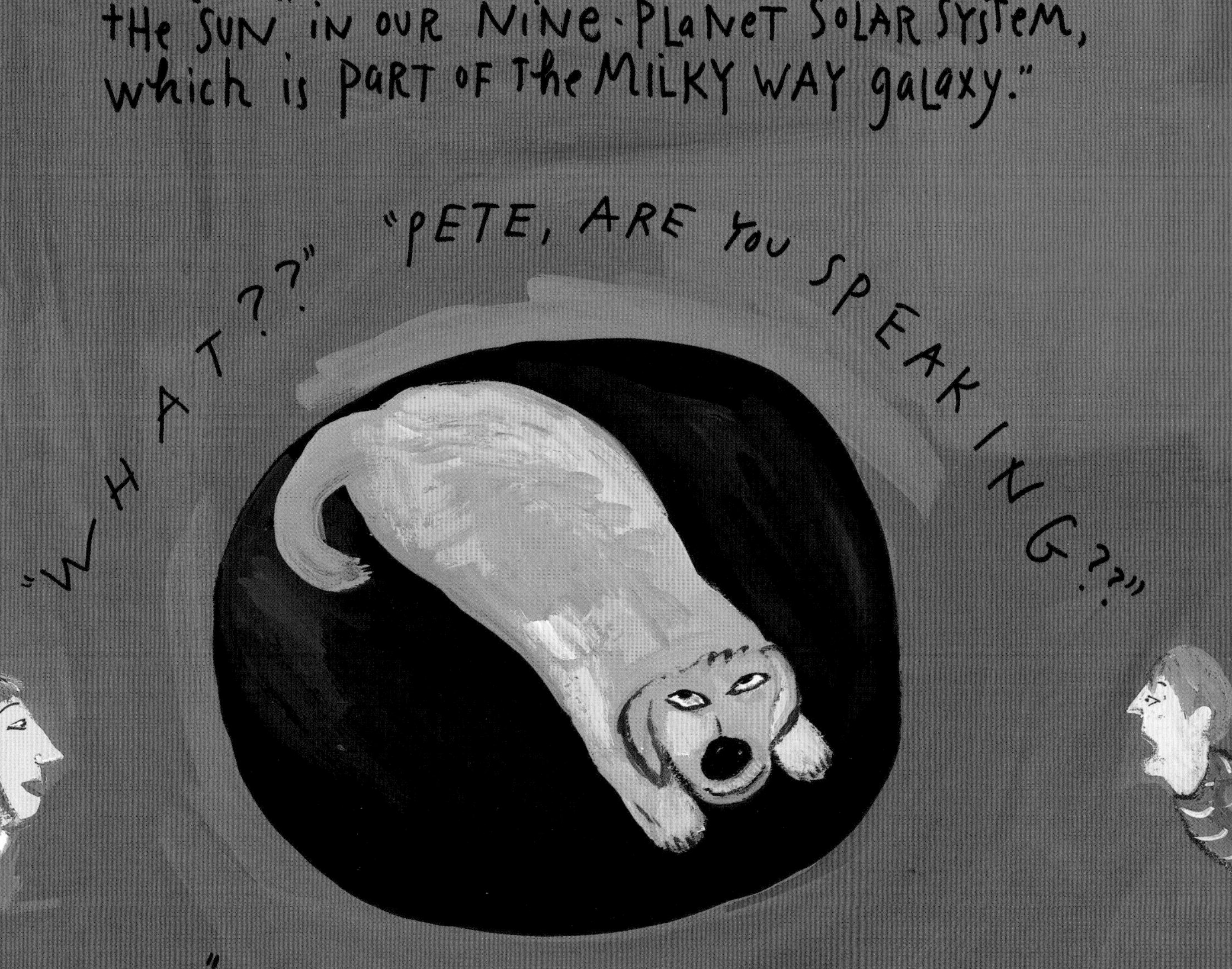

"OBVIOUSLY YOU DO NOT expect ME TO Be a SENTIENT BEING, BUT EMPIRICALLY SPeaKING, YOU CANNOT DENY THAT I am speaking. ERGO, I am SPeaKING."

(WE DID NOT UNDERSTAND ONE WORD OF THAT.)

Pete Explained, "I ATe the ENCYCLOPEDIA AND I am ReaLLY SMART."

He told us about

FloRa

(pLANTS)

and

FauNa (ANIMaLS).

He explained

GRaVITY

and he

was veRY

GRave.

He toLD us aBout the GUMDROP MOUNTAINS IN CHINA.

He told us who

INvented PResents.

He explained

how A

Lightbulb

works and what a

SHRew eATS

aND WHY a PeRSON CRieS

(and Believe Me, there are SO MANY Reasons a peRSON CRieS that it would take Three oR FouR Books to List ALL the Reasons).

We were so excited that we decided to sneak Pete back to school disguised as our cousin Pearl Buttonweiser.

Milton thought Pearl looked familiar, but he thought, "I am just a bird. What do I know?"

We WENT to English with MR. DIVIDAR DIVECKY, who WORSHIPS the THESAURUS. He says things like, "If by chance (serendipity, luck) you FIND a legitimate (VALID, RATIONAL) Reason to EAT (devour, CONSUME) a RADISH, tHEN BY all Means, DO SO."

How great is THAT?

Pete recited a poem by Gertrude Stein.

"Did he did we
did we and did he
did he did he
did did he
did did did
he did did he did."

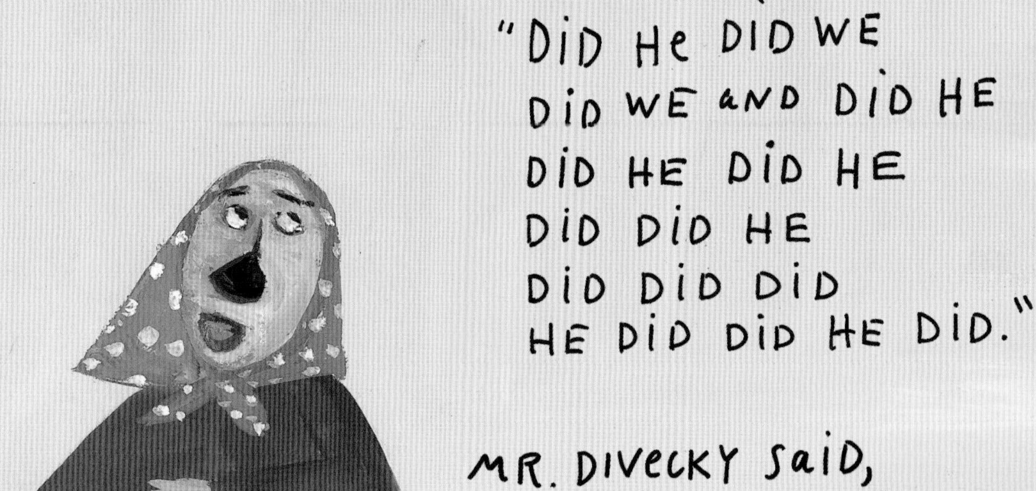

Mr. Divecky said, "You may think Gertrude Stein is crazy (insane, nuts, delirious, cuckoo), but I love her dearly."

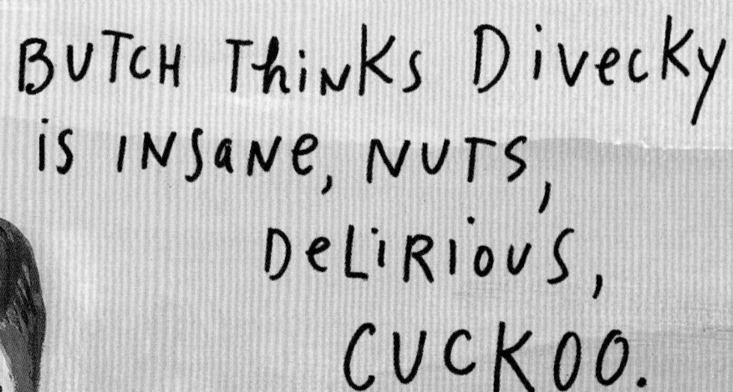

Butch thinks Divecky is insane, nuts, delirious, cuckoo.

But I love Divecky dearly.

BACK IN MATH, MR. SPITZER WAS TALKING ABOUT PENTAGONAL PYRAMIDS AND TRIANGULAR PRISMS, WHICH REMINDED ME OF RAINBOWS, WHICH REMINDED ME OF FLYING A KITE ON A BREEZY DAY
when FROM FAR AWAY I heard
"POPPY WISE, STOP DAYDREAMING."
"I'M STILL IN THIS BOX."
FRACTIONS
PETE SAID, "what is WRONG with a Reverie filled with pleasing visions?"
MR. SPITZER STARED AT PETE. HE NOTICED A WAGGING TAIL. HE SMELLED A RAT. MR. SPITZER WAS NO DUMMY. "IS PEARL BUTTONWEISER PETE THE DOG?
TO MISS HONEYBEE. NOW."

We all went to Miss Honeybee to SPILL the BEANS.

Pete apologized to Mr. Spitzer a million, billion, trillion times. (That is a lot of times.)

Mr. Spitzer started to

SMILE.

Miss Honeybee stared out the window, which is an EXCELLENT way to THINK, and said,

"Rules are sometimes meant to be broken. PETE MAY STAY."

The REST of the DAY PETE was the STAR of the SCHOOL.

We DID NOT Have to SAY ONE WORD.
PETE answered EVERY QUESTION.
"A REGULAR EINSTEIN."
THERE WAS NO BETTER DOG OR BETTER DAY IN SCHOOL.

That night we actually looked forward to doing our homework.

"Pete, what is the smallest mammal on Earth?"

Pete looked BLANK.

"PETE, WHAT is a trapezoid?"

Pete looked BLANKER.

"Pete, what is a gerund?" Nothing.

"Pete, what is the Bill of Rights?" ZIP!

Pete was no longer speaking. Pete was CLUELESS!!!

He had DIGESTED all the INFORMATION and it was no longer in him. Pete was back to being dear SWEET PETE.

It had been an AMAZING DAY. I had learned MANY things. I learned that the DODO BIRD is extinct. I learned that people STILL eat liverwurst. That if I ran a SCHOOL, you would get extra credit for daydreaming. That there is no end to learning. You could say it is INFINITE. That sometimes people who are STRICT turn out to be NICE and people you CAN'T STAND can be interesting. That SCHOOL is like LIFE with GOOD days and BAD days and that you NEVER EVER KNOW when you LEAST expect it, you will have a

PLEASE GET A SHEET OF PAPER AND A PEN OR A

1. WHAT IS THE NAME OF THIS BOOK?
2. WHAT IS YOUR NAME? ARE YOU SURE?
3. WHAT IS IT ABOUT MATH?
4. WHAT DID YOU HAVE FOR BREAKFAST THIS MORNING?
5. WHAT IS THE SMALLEST MAMMAL ON EARTH?
6. I WASN'T PAYING ATTENTION DURING QUESTION 2. WHAT IS YOUR NAME?

QUIZ!

PENCIL AND WE WILL HAVE A POP POP POP QUIZ. HA!

7. HOW MANY TIMES DID THE WORD "DID" APPEAR ON THE DIVIDAR DIVECKY PAGE?

8. WHICH WORDS ARE MADE UP?

9. WHAT COLOR ARE MISS HONEYBEE'S SHOES? WHAT COLOR ARE MR. SPITZER'S SHOES? EXTRA CREDIT: DO YOU THINK THAT MR. SPITZER AND MISS HONEYBEE COULD EVER FALL IN LOVE? IF THE IDEA IS TOO AWFUL, FORGET I ASKED.

10. HOW MANY MISTAKES DID YOU MAKE TODAY? PLEASE WRITE YOUR NAME ON A PIECE OF PAPER AND LIST MISTAKES MADE TODAY IN DETAIL AND SEND TO MAIRA KALMAN

℅ PUTNAM 345 HUDSON ST.
NEW YORK, N.Y. 10014

IF YOU DIDN'T MAKE ANY MISTAKES TODAY, I WILL EAT MY SHOES! (JUST LIKE PETE.)

SOME Things NOT in this BOOK.
I don't Know.
Grey Lag-Goose
great spotted Cuckoo
Tawny Pipit
A Box of Eggs.
My Favorite Monkey Bowl that Nobody likes.
Pete's Dear Friend Harry.
A Beautiful Box made by the Beautiful Lulu.
A piece of a cardboard chair. that you-Know-Who Ate.
A well-loved paint brush.